Teggs is no ordinary dinosaur –
he's an **ASTROSAUR!** Captain of
the amazing spaceship DSS *Sauropod*,
he goes on dangerous missions and
fights evil – along with his faithful
crew, Gipsy, Arx and Iggy!

Visit the BRAND NEW Astrosaurs
website for games, downloads,
competitions and the chance to
meet the crew and find out your
astrosaur name!
www.astrosaurs.co.uk

D0112269

Read all the adventures of Teggs, Blink and Dutch!

DESTINATION: DANGER!
CONTEST CARNAGE!

Read Teggs's adventures as a real ASTROSAUR!

Find out more at www.astrosaurs.co.uk

Astrosaurs ACADEMY
STEVE COLE

DESTINATION: DANGER!
Illustrated by Woody Fox

RED FOX

DESTINATION: DANGER!
A RED FOX BOOK 978 1 862 30553 3

First published in Great Britain by Red Fox,
an imprint of Random House Children's Books
A Random House Group Company

This edition published 2008

5 7 9 10 8 6

The Random House Group Limited supports the Forest Stewardship Council (FSC),
the leading international forest certification organization. All our titles that are printed on
Greenpeace-approved FSC-certified paper carry the FSC logo. Our paper procurement
policy can be found at www.rbooks.co.uk/environment.

Set in 16pt Bembo

Red Fox Books are published by Random House Children's Books,
61–63 Uxbridge Road, London W5 5SA

www.**kids**at**randomhouse**.co.uk
www.**rbooks**.co.uk

Addresses for companies within The Random House Group Limited can be found at:
www.randomhouse.co.uk/offices.htm

THE RANDOM HOUSE GROUP Limited Reg. No. 954009

A CIP catalogue record for this book is available from the British Library.

Printed in the UK by CPI Bookmarque, Croydon, CR0 4TD

For Tobey and Amy

WELCOME TO THE COOLEST SCHOOL IN SPACE . . .

Most people think that dinosaurs are extinct. Most people believe that these weird and wondrous reptiles were wiped out when a massive space rock smashed into the Earth, 65 million years ago.

HA! What do *they* know? The dinosaurs were way cleverer than anyone thought . . .

This is what *really* happened: they saw that big lump of space rock coming, and when it became clear that dino-life could not survive such a terrible crash, the dinosaurs all took off in huge, dung-powered spaceships before the rock hit.

They set their sights on the stars and left the Earth, never to return . . .

Now, 65 million years later, both plant-eaters and meat-eaters have built massive empires in space. But the carnivores are never happy unless they're causing 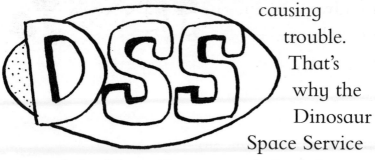 trouble. That's why the Dinosaur Space Service needs herbivore heroes to defend the Vegetarian Sector. Such heroes have a special name. They are called ASTROSAURS.

But you can't change from a dinosaur to an astrosaur overnight. It takes years of training on the special planet of Astro Prime in a *very* special place . . . the Astrosaurs Academy! It's a sensational space school where manic missions and incredible adventures are the only subjects! The academy's doors are always open, but only to the bravest, boldest dinosaurs . . .

And to YOU!

NOTE: One of the most famous astrosaurs of all is Captain Teggs Stegosaur. This staggering stegosaurus is the star of many stories . . . But before he became a spaceship captain, he was a cadet at Astrosaurs Academy. These are the adventures of the young Teggs and his friends — adventures that made him the dinosaur he is today!

Talking Dinosaur!

How to say the prehistoric names in
DESTINATION: DANGER!

STEGOSAURUS – *STEG-oh-SORE-us*

GRYPOSAURUS – *GRIPE-oh-SORE-us*

DIPLODOCUS – *di-PLOH-de-kus*

IGUANODON – *ig-WA-noh-don*

DICERATOPS – *dye-SERRA-tops*

TRICERATOPS – *try-SERRA-tops*

PTEROSAUR – *teh-roh-SORE*

SEISMOSAURUS – *SIZE-moh-SORE-us*

ANKYLOSAUR – *an-KILE-oh-SORE*

DRYOSAURUS – *DRY-oh-SORE-us*

LAMBEOSAUR – *LAMB-ee-oh-SORE*

SAUROPELTA – *SORE-oh-PEL-ta*

The cadets

THE DARING DINOS

Teggs   Dutch   Blink

DAMONA'S DARLINGS

Damona   Netta   Splatt

Chapter One

A DINOSAUR'S DREAM

Teggs Stegosaur sat on the back seat of the space-bus, eating his thirty-seventh packed lunch of the day.

And it wasn't even noon yet!

Teggs was a young, orange-brown stegosaurus, who was handsome, bright and very often hungry. He got even hungrier when he was excited . . .

And right now, he was more excited than he had ever been in his life!

"Are we nearly there yet?" Teggs called to the bus driver.

"That's the five hundredth time you've asked," said the bus driver, a grumpy gryposaurus. "And the answer's still no. We only left an hour ago!"

Teggs shrugged and tucked into another sack of apples. As he munched, he stared out of the window at distant stars and comets twinkling in the darkness. He had always dreamed of flying through space, helping other dinosaurs and having adventures. And now, here he was on an empty, rickety old bus hoping to make his dreams come true . . .

 It was millions of years since dinosaurs had left behind the planet Earth to start a new life among the stars. Now they lived in a part of space called the Jurassic Quadrant. The plant-eaters lived on one side and the meat-eaters lived on the other.

But sometimes fights broke out, or spooky space monsters attacked, or innocent leaf-munchers needed help. When that happened, special, daring, space-travelling dinosaurs zoomed to the rescue. They belonged to the Dinosaur Space Service and called themselves *astrosaurs*.

More than anything, Teggs wanted to become an astrosaur too. But first I've got to prove I have what it takes, he thought — by training at the Astrosaurs Academy!

3

"Are we nearly there yet?" Teggs asked yet again.

"*No!*" the driver yelled back, as a large grey planet loomed up in the bus window. "Our next stop is the planet Diplox."

"Diplox," said Teggs, thinking hard. Astrosaurs had to know the names of every planet in the Jurassic Quadrant, as well as the dinosaurs that lived there. "Isn't that where diplodocus come from?"

"Correct," said the driver. He stopped the bus at the orbiting bus stop and opened the doors. "And here comes one now."

A dark green dinosaur wriggled through the bus doors with a huge rucksack on his back. He was short for a diplodocus, but very sturdy. He looked around the bus, his long neck swishing this way and that.

Then he saw Teggs and smiled. "Hey, dude!"

"Hi! I'm Teggs," said Teggs.

"Dutch Delaney," replied the small diplodocus. "Good to meet you, Teggs." He pulled a bat and ball from his rucksack with his mouth. "Do you like sports?"

Teggs grinned. "Let's play!"

Dutch knocked the ball over to Teggs, who whacked it with his spiky tail. But he hit it too hard and it started bouncing all over the bus! "Cool!" cried Dutch, as he dodged the ball with amazing skill.

5

Finally, the ball hit the driver on the head. "Ow!" he shouted. "No ball games allowed on this bus!"

"Sorry!" Teggs and Dutch called together – but they couldn't help laughing.

"That was a great shot, Teggs," said Dutch admiringly.

Teggs smiled. "That was nice dodging, Dutch!"

"Thanks," said Dutch. "Been on the bus long?"

"Bean? Where's a bean?" Teggs looked

around ravenously, licking his lips.

"No, dude," said Dutch quickly. "I meant, have you been riding this bus a long time?"

"Oh! Only an hour or two," Teggs told him. "I'm on my way to the planet Astro Prime to join—"

"The Astrosaurs Academy!" Dutch beamed. "Me too! Wow, this is awesome." He pulled his 'welcome' letter from his rucksack. "You know, I'm down to share a room with a stegosaurus. I hope he's as cool as you . . ."

"That's funny," said Teggs, looking at his own letter. "I think I'm sharing with a diplodocus . . ."

They both re-read what the letters said – and gasped.

"I'm sharing with *you*!" Teggs cried.

"And me with you!" Dutch happily shook hands with Teggs. "It says we have to share with a flying reptile too."

"Maybe he'll get on at the next stop!" said Teggs, opening up his thirty-eighth packed lunch of apples and ferns. "Would you like something to eat while we're waiting, Dutch?"

"Thanks, dude, but my mum already packed me a snack."
Dutch pulled out an enormous, tasty-looking tree from his rucksack.
"Want a bite?"

Teggs grinned.
"Dutch, I think you might be the perfect roommate. Astrosaurs Academy, here we come!"

Chapter Two

IN TROUBLE ALREADY!

Now Teggs had made friends with
Dutch, the long bus journey seemed to
whizz by. More and more dinosaurs got
on board at every stop, all on their way
to Astrosaurs Academy – but no flying
reptiles were among them. The bus was
bulging with bodies by the time Astro
Prime came in sight!

From a distance, the planet looked
like a red and green
ball floating in
space. But as the
bus zoomed closer
Teggs could see it
was a real patchwork

of places. Huge sweeping deserts mixed with lush jungles. Frozen ice fields gave way to stony sweeps of wilderness. Deep, orange oceans lapped at every different shore.

And on a blue island at the planet's equator stood the Astrosaurs Academy!

"*Wow*," said Teggs, as he and Dutch peered out of the window. "So this is our new home while we're training!"

The bus soared over the academy, and soon everyone on board was chattering excitedly. It was as if a school had been built in the middle of a massive adventure camp. Teggs's eyes lit up as he saw playing fields, an assault course, a water park and an athletics track, as well as launch pads for spaceships and astro-jets.

Dutch pointed to a huddle of huge wooden huts, hugging the earth like giant woodlice. "What are they?"

Teggs checked his guidebook. "They are the dino-dorms. All the students live there." He pointed to another building. "And there's the best place of all – the canteen!"

The bus landed outside a gleaming metal pyramid. An iguanodon wearing the red uniform of an astrosaur instructor was waiting for them.

"Pay attention, you lot!" the instructor shouted. "Welcome to Astrosaurs Academy. You are just in time – your head teacher, Commander Gruff, is about to speak to all new cadets in the main hall. Grab yourselves a uniform and move out!"

"Let's go!" cried Teggs.

They waved goodbye to the bus driver. Then they ran across the springy blue grass and joined the stream of excited dinosaurs pouring into the pyramid.

The first thing Teggs and Dutch came to was an enormous changing room. Astrosaur cadets wore deep blue tops with 'AA' written on the front and a golden leaf on one sleeve. Clothes flew through the air as every dinosaur tried to find an outfit that fitted.

Proudly wearing their new uniforms, Teggs and Dutch followed the signs to the main hall. But when

they got there, they found a crowd outside listening to a large, red diceratops. She had two big horns, three big brown freckles on each cheek – and one very big mouth!

"Of course, my Uncle Hiro is a famous astrosaur captain," she said, preening herself. "He's taken me to *loads* of amazing planets . . ."

"Wow," said a wide-eyed triceratops. "You're so cool, Damona!"

"I was even there when he fought four hundred T. rexes at the Battle of Belliflopp!" Damona went on.

"Really?" A yellow pterosaur with quizzical eyes, glasses and a soft voice hopped up to her. "I read that there were only two hundred T. rexes on Belliflopp."

"Who cares what you read, beak-face?" said Damona hotly. "*I* know because *I* was there. It was definitely four hundred!"

"Then perhaps you can't count!" said Teggs, stepping between them. "I recorded a TV programme about the battle. Your uncle said there was one T. rex hiding on every island in the Belliflopp Sea – making two hundred in total!" He pulled his laptop from his rucksack. "Would you like to watch the show and see?"

Some of the crowd started to snigger. Damona blushed and glared at Teggs. Then she flounced away into the main hall.

"What a silly show-off," said Dutch.

"Maybe it's just her way of making friends," said Teggs, turning to the pterosaur. "I'm Teggs, and this is Dutch. Are you OK?"

"Teggs? Dutch?" The dino-bird,
blinked several times, then grinned.
"Wow! I think I'm sharing a dino-dorm
with you. My name's Blink Fingawing."

"So *you're* our other roommate!"
Dutch grinned.

"This is great," said Teggs happily.

Then the ground started to shake under
their feet. "Uh-oh. I think Commander
Gruff is on his way."

Teggs, Dutch and Blink rushed inside
and found some seats in the middle of
the hall – just as Commander Gruff

thumped onto the large stage at the front. He was a giant green seismosaurus. Gruff had fought a thousand space battles – and had the scars to prove it. But now he had retired from the DSS to teach young astrosaur cadets.

"All right, you horrible lot!" he growled, chewing on an unripe banana as if it was a cigar. "Right now, you are simply dinosaurs. But if you train hard, you might just become *astrosaurs*!"

The cadets clapped loudly.

"You must be brave!" said Commander Gruff. "You must have guts!"

Teggs patted his tummy and smiled at Dutch and Blink. "I've got lots of guts."

"You must be hungry for victory!" Gruff shouted.

Just then, Teggs's tummy gave a huge rumble and the whole hall burst out laughing.

"NO ONE DISTURBS MY SPEECHES!" bellowed Gruff. He stretched his neck all the way to the middle of the hall and glared down at Teggs. "What's your name, cadet?"

"Um . . . Teggs, sir," said Teggs, his heart sinking.

"Get out!" Gruff barked. "I'll see you later."

Teggs felt everyone staring as he got up and plodded from the hall. Damona stuck out her tongue as he passed, and his cheeks blushed bright red. Only here five minutes, he thought, and I'm in trouble already!

But just as he reached the front of the hall, there was an almighty crash above the stage – and part of the ceiling started to fall in!

Commander Gruff jumped away as a giant, struggling monster forced its way through the hole and dropped to the stage below with a *THUMP*. Teggs stared in horror as the monster reared up, roaring with rage and baring its savage teeth . . .

There was a *T. rex* in the heart of the Astrosaurs Academy!

Chapter Three

THE DARING DINOS

Panic broke out in the hall. Dinosaurs jumped up, yelling in alarm as the enormous meat-eater stomped towards them. Commander Gruff reared up to face the T. rex, but it grabbed his neck and threw him to the ground with a *CRASH*.

"Commander!" Teggs yelled. But Gruff didn't move. "Dutch, Blink, look after him. I'll try to hold off the T. rex."

"Everyone out!" shouted Damona, shooing people towards the doors. "Quickly and calmly! No squashing!"

While Damona cleared the hall and Dutch and Blink tried to drag Gruff out of danger, Teggs ran towards the monster. "Take *this*, meathead!" he cried, whacking the T. rex on the knee with his spiky tail.

The T. rex growled and tried to bite Teggs – but then a speeding baseball bounced off its nose and stopped it in its tracks.

"Got you!" Dutch whooped. He pulled more baseballs from his rucksack and started lobbing them at the monster's head.

Meanwhile, Blink flew up into the air. He flapped around like a mad moth with wind, pecking the T. rex in the ear. At the same time, Teggs stamped on its foot. The T. rex didn't know who to squish first!

"Hey! I've found a wire in its ear!"
yelled Blink, tugging out a bright red
lead. Sparks began to fly from the
monster's eyeballs.

"It must be a robot!" Teggs realized.
"But where did it come from?"

"Out of my way, you lot," said Damona. She had finished getting everyone outside. Now she lowered her horns and charged at the sparking T. rex. *WHAM!* She hit it so hard that both its legs fell off! With a clanking, clanging *KER-KROOM!* the robot broke down.

"Well done, Damona!" said Teggs. "That was some charge!"

"It was, wasn't it?" she agreed. "I suppose you were quite brave too."

"You all were," said Commander Gruff, getting up again. "Well done, cadets.

You handled that exercise very well."

"Exercise?" Teggs echoed.

"I *love* exercise!" said Dutch.

"The commander means it was just a test, silly!" said Damona.

"Exactly," Gruff agreed. "The first thing I do with any new group of cadets is test how they respond to deadly danger."

Blink polished his glasses on his wing. "I suppose that if you want to be an astrosaur, you must expect the unexpected!"

"Too right." Gruff turned to Damona. "You got everyone out double-quick, cadet. Now let's see you get them back in again!"

"Yes, sir!" Damona saluted, then ran out to round up the other students.

"And as for you, Teggs . . ." Gruff pulled a clump of ferns from the wall and gave them to him.

"Keep your tummy rumbles under control and sit back down."

Teggs scoffed the ferns, saluted and went back to his seat with Blink and Dutch. "Phew!" he said.

Soon all the cadets were back inside, staring at the wreck of the robot T. rex.

"That was just a little test of your bravery," Gruff growled. "And let me tell you – if you ever meet a *real* T. rex, screaming and shouting will *not* help you!" He chomped some more on his unripe banana. "Now it's time to talk about your first mission."

Blink blinked excitedly. "Wow! A mission already!"

"As you know, astrosaurs are excellent explorers – and so must you be," Gruff bellowed. "SO! You will get into teams of three. First thing tomorrow morning you will be taken to the land of Quarrik. It is a deserted wilderness. Each team must build a camp and then go off to explore. To win your Planet Explorer medals, you must find something extraordinary and rare and bring it back to the academy for a show-and-tell. The best one will win a special award."

"How long do we have, sir?" called Damona.

"Twenty-four hours," said Gruff. "You will camp out overnight and an astro-jet will pick you up the next morning. But until then you will be completely on your own."

"Awesome!" whispered Dutch, and

Teggs and Blink both nodded.

"Class dismissed," said Gruff. "But before you go, you horrible lot . . . you can clean up the mess this robot made and fix that hole in the roof!"

Later, tired and covered in dust and dirt, Teggs, Blink and Dutch staggered back to the dino-dorms. Their room was large but quite bare. The only furniture was two beds and a large nest, three desks, three wardrobes, a couch and a fridge.

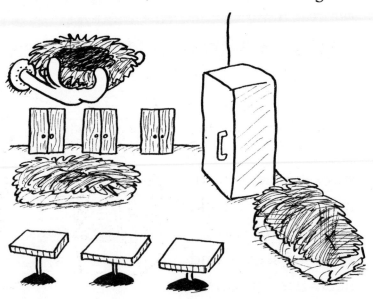

"The fridge could be larger," said Teggs.

"Eh?" Blink blinked. "It's the size of a shuttle!"

"Exactly!" said Dutch. "But we've got *starship*-sized appetites!"

"Well, we had better get unpacking." Teggs struggled to pull a large bush out of his bag. "I've got so much food in here I should call it a ruck*snack*!"

"I'll give you a hand," said Dutch. He took an enormous leafy bite. "Or do I mean a mouth!"

"Hey!" Teggs grinned. "Save me a bit. Go and eat Blink's grub."

"Yes, I've got a nice crunchy bug salad here," said Blink. He stuck his beak in a lunchbox and sucked up a big pile of speckled leaves and deep-fried insects.

"Mmm! Care for a pickled earwig?"

Dutch pulled a face. "Maybe I'll pass."

The three new friends explored the rest of the room. Blink flapped into his nest and neatly arranged each stray stick.

Teggs bounced on his bed, testing the springs.

Meanwhile, Dutch opened his bag and started chucking his clothes carelessly over his shoulder.

A huge pair of pants landed on Blink's head. "Oof!" he twittered. "What are you doing?"

"Unpacking, dude," said Dutch.

"But you're making such a mess!" Blink grinned. "Brilliant! I love sorting out messes!" And as Dutch went on emptying his bag, Blink swooped about the room, catching things and folding them neatly. "I think I'm definitely going to like it here," he cried, blinking busily away. "New uniforms, new friends . . . and we've had our first battle already!"

"Speaking of the battle," said Teggs. "I thought we made a pretty good team against that robot. So I was wondering . . ."

"Would we like to be on your team for the mission tomorrow?" Blink looked at Dutch and they both nodded. "Yes, please!"

"That would be way cool!" Dutch added.

"Excellent!" said Teggs, jumping off the bed. "I bet we will find something amazing in the wilderness."

Dutch nodded. "And build a brilliant camp too!"

"But what shall we call ourselves?" Blink wondered.

"I know," Teggs declared. "The Daring Dinos!"

"*Awwwwwwesome!*" roared Dutch. "Now let's celebrate by eating ten dinners in the canteen!" He held out his hand. "Do we dare?"

Teggs and Blink put their hands on top of his and they all shouted together: "WE DARE!"

Whooping, the Daring Dinos raced outside. As they ran over the blue grass, Teggs saw a shooting star fall from the sky. His mum had always said you were supposed to wish on a falling star, so Teggs did.

"I wish that the Planet Explorer mission tomorrow is the wildest mission ever!" he said.

The shooting star lingered in the sky for a few moments, almost as if it was listening. Then it dropped out of sight behind the distant mountains.

Little did Teggs know that his wish was going to come true — but not in a way that anyone could expect . . .

Chapter Four

JOURNEY TO PERIL

At sunrise the next day, all the astrosaur cadets trooped down to the launch pads to collect their camping kits and get on the astro-jets.

Blink was super-excited. He was zipping about like a budgie with a firework up its bottom. "A mission!" he cried. "Our very first astro-tastic mission!"

Teggs grinned through a yawn. He had spent most of the night checking his alarm clock to see if it was time to get up yet. He couldn't wait to get started.

Dutch had barely slept either. Now he was actually sleepwalking to the astro-jets, snoring like an elephant!

Suddenly, a pink ankylosaur with a blue bow tied around her big, club-like tail sneaked up behind him and shouted, "BOO!"

Dutch jumped in the air in surprise, and his rucksack fell off his back. It landed on Teggs's toe. "*Ow!*"

Teggs and Dutch both glared at the ankylosaur, whose bumpy body quivered as she giggled away. Damona walked up to her with a big smile. "Good trick, Netta. You really made the diplodocus jump!"

"I'll make you jump in a minute!" Dutch retorted.

But suddenly, a small, nimble boy dinosaur with the head of a turtle and the tail of a snake went zooming over Dutch's back and made him jump again!
Damona and Netta laughed even louder. "Nice one, Splatt!"

"So this is *your* team, is it, Damona?" asked Teggs.

"Meet Damona's Darlings," she replied. "Netta is super-strong and Splatt is a super-speedy dryosaurus. We are going to be the best team at Astrosaurs Academy."

"No contest!" said Splatt, whizzing around Dutch in a circle.

Dutch tried to sit on him, but missed and sat on a big thistle. "*Ouch!*"

Blink came flapping down beside Damona. "I think you'll find that we are the best team, actually," he said proudly. "The Daring Dinos!"

"The Dino Dimwits, more like!" Damona laughed. She walked off with Netta and Splatt. "See you in the wilderness, boys!"

Dutch scowled. "Dudes, I think those three could be trouble."

"Good." Teggs grinned. "I *like* trouble." He put an arm round Blink and his tail round Dutch. "Now, let's get on board and get ready to win that special prize. Do we dare?"

"WE DARE!" they yelled together.

The astro-jets took off and soared away through the bright blue sky. In minutes, the academy was just a speck in the distance.

The dinosaurs were all squashed in together with their camping kits, ready to parachute down to the surface once they reached the drop zone. They flew over an orange sea and a range of purple mountains. Then Teggs saw the land beneath them grow grey and grotty. Soon there was nothing to see but bare hillsides and stony plains and the occasional twisted tree.

"We have now reached the land of
Quarrik," Blink announced like a tour
guide. "I read about it in a book. It's five
hundred miles north of the academy,
west of the Backplate Sea. There are
loads of really interesting caves—"

"Put a sock in your beak!" called
Netta, and some of the cadets laughed.

Blink looked sad.

"Don't worry about them, Blink," said Teggs. "If they don't want to know that's their problem. What else is in Quarrik?"

"There are some very steep cliffs and very deep valleys," Blink went on, perking up a bit. "I hope we get to explore some of those!"

The astro-jet started to slow down and a red light flashed above their heads. "I think we've reached the drop zone," Teggs realized.

"And I want to jump first!" Dutch declared, as a hatch opened up in the side of the jet.

He lumbered over and jumped out without a second thought. "*Awwwwwwwwwe-soooooome!*" he yelled.

"Me next!" cried Damona and Teggs together. They squeezed out through the hatch and dived into empty space.

"*Whoaaaa!*" yelled Teggs in delight.

Here he was – a
six-ton stegosaurus
– flying like
a dino-bird!
Soon, the sky
was full of
dinosaurs plunging
downwards.
They opened their
parachutes and
floated to earth
as gently as leaves
in the autumn.

"*Wow!*" Teggs shouted, as he hit the ground beside Dutch. The parachute fell over him like a stripy cloak. "Let's do it again!"

"No time for that," squawked Blink, landing beside them. He hadn't needed a parachute, of course. "We must find a cool place to camp."

Already, the other cadets were zooming over the wasteland, as busy as ants, hunting about for the best places. Blink led the way up a hill, poking his beak here and there. "I'm glad I read that guidebook now. Somewhere around here there's a really good cave . . ."

Teggs bounded to the top of the hill. "How about this one?" he said.

Blink flapped over to see. "That's it! This will give us extra shelter."

Dutch beamed. "And it's close to that little stream for drinking water and washing too! Top work, Blink!"

But suddenly, they heard a cry for help from further down the hill. "Somebody . . . come quick!"

Dutch frowned. "That sounds like Damona!"

Teggs pointed. "There!"

Damona was lying under a fallen tree. Netta was struggling to lift it so her friend could get free.

"Looks like she's in trouble," yelled Teggs. "Come on!"

Chapter Five

A DEADLY DISCOVERY

Teggs ran down the hill to help, with
Blink and Dutch close behind.
"Damona, are you all right?"

"Yes, thanks!" She sucked in her
tummy and wriggled out from under
the tree. "Fancy that! I seem to have got
out all by myself . . ."

"And *I've* found a *brilliant* place to camp!" called Splatt from the top of the hill. He put down his self-inflating tent right outside the cave Teggs had just spotted!

"Unfair, dude," said Dutch crossly. "We were there first!"

"You should have stayed there then, shouldn't you?" Damona and Netta waved and laughed. "So long, see you, wouldn't want to be you!"

Blink blinked furiously. "The cheats!"

Dutch scowled. "That was *our* camp."

"Oh, let them have it," said Teggs. He turned and walked off in the opposite direction. "I bet we'll find a much better place to camp over here."

"Maybe." Blink didn't seem sure. "The guidebook says there are lots of steep cliffs and deep valleys this way."

"Well, we're bound to find some brilliant things for show-and-tell as we go," said Dutch. "Keep your eyes peeled, Blink!"

Blink flew on ahead, circling above the trees and peeping behind big rocks. But it seemed all the best places had been taken.

"Look! There's a giant pine cone!" Dutch picked it up. "Pretty unusual, huh?"

"I've seen two teams with giant pine cones already," said Blink.

Dutch tried again. "What about this funny-shaped twig?"

"I've seen *three* teams with funny-shaped twigs."

They rambled onwards, for hours and hours, until they were far away from everyone else. They scrambled up steep slopes and splashed through muddy mountain streams.

Teggs paused by a tree full of hazelnuts. "What about these?"

Blink frowned. "Nuts? For show-and-tell?"

"No, for a snack!" said Teggs, shaking

the tree and catching the nuts in his mouth. "I'm starving!"

They plodded along beside a cliff edge then took a winding woodland path. A cold wind started to blow up. It whistled eerily through

the branches of the twisted trees. The
howls of strange creatures echoed in the
distance.

Dutch gulped, a little bit spooked. "I
don't like this."

"Maybe we should make a camp
right here," Teggs suggested.

Blink quickly agreed. "I have a feeling
there's something really unusual around
here just waiting to be
discovered."

"Yeah!" said
Dutch. He
pulled an
orange
inflatable
bundle from
his rucksack
and laid it on
the ground.
"Luckily it won't take long to set up
camp. These tents are self-inflating – all
you do is pull the string and up they go!"

He bent over the bundle and yanked on a long black cord. The tent puffed up in moments to the size of a garage. But then a strong gust of wind caught it and the tent blew away!

"Oh, no!" yelled Dutch. "My tent! I can't sleep without it, my toes will freeze off!"

"Come on, Dutch," said Blink, flapping his leathery wings. "I'll help you catch it!"

"I'll stay here and get the campfire going," Teggs told them. "Good luck!"

The squashy orange tent was blown tumbling through the sky like an oversized kite. Dutch charged after it, crashing through bracken and leaping over rocks. Blink flapped his wings and tried to overtake it.

"Quickly!" the pterosaur cried. "It looks like the edge of the cliff up ahead. If the tent blows over there we'll never get it back!"

Dutch broke into a gallop. Stretching his neck as far as it would go, he grabbed hold of the runaway tent with his teeth. At the same time, Blink dive-bombed it, pinning it to the ground with his claws – just before it reached the cliff edge.

"Thanks, dude!" said Dutch, spitting out his rubbery mouthful. "That was close!"

"Shh!" said Blink, sniffing the air. "What's that horrible smell?"

"It's not me!" Dutch grinned. "Whoever smelt it, dealt it!"

"I'm serious." Blink's beak was twitching. "Yuck! It smells like maggots and muck and mouldy barbecues . . ."

"And it's coming from over the cliff edge," Dutch realized.

Cautiously, the two friends crept over to the ledge to see. And what they saw chilled their blood.

A small crimson spaceship had crashed in the valley below. Six huge, evil-looking monsters in dark tatty clothes were stamping through the wreckage. Their legs were huge but their arms were tiny. The cold sunlight caught on their claws and their rows of knife-sharp teeth.

Both Dutch and Blink recognized the monsters at once.

T. rexes!

Chapter Six

THE TRICK AND THE T. REX

"This can't be happening!" Dutch stared at Blink. "What are T. rexes doing on Astro Prime?"

"Maybe Commander Gruff is testing us again," Blink whispered hopefully. "Maybe they're robots like before!"

But suddenly, they heard the tallest T. rex speak in an angry roar. "Will ship fly again, pilot?"

"No, Lord Slyme," growled a T. rex in flying goggles. "Ship completely stuffed."

"But me on way to space-car races!" Lord Slyme hissed. "Now me have to miss them. Me go back to spaceship shop and EAT owner for selling me pile of scrap!"

"First us must call rescue ship from Teerex Major," said another T. rex.

Dutch gulped. "Dude, I don't think those things are Gruff's robots. They're meat, not metal."

Blink nodded nervously. "I read that a T. rex noble-saur always travels with five servants. Their spaceship must have gone off course and crashed here!"

"Me STARVING," roared Slyme suddenly.

Another T. rex held up an arm. "Please be eating my unworthy elbow, Lord."

But Slyme swatted his servant's arm away. "No!" He sniffed the air, looking

up towards where Blink and Dutch were hiding. "Me smell fresh, soft meat . . . Nice smell, coming from south . . . Us find."

Shaking with fear, Blink and Dutch slithered away out of sight.

"What can we do?" hissed Dutch. "If those things go south, they will sniff out the cadets' campsites for sure."

"We must tell Teggs," said Blink, blinking so fast his eyelids were a blur through his glasses. "Together we can work out a plan . . . I hope!"

Teggs was just collecting firewood when Dutch and Blink came hurtling towards him, dragging the torn tent between them. They were red-faced, wild-eyed and gasping for breath. Dutch panted so hard he blew away Teggs's pile of sticks!

"What's up?" Teggs asked.

"What's *down*, you mean," puffed Blink, fanning his hot face with his wing. "A T. rex ship, to be precise!"

Dutch nodded. "There are six real live T. rexes on our doorstep!"

"*What . . . ?*" Struck dumb with amazement, Teggs listened as his friends revealed all they had seen and heard.

"That shooting star I saw last night," he remembered. "It must have been the T. rex ship crash-landing here." Teggs jumped to his feet. "Everyone in Quarrik is in terrible danger!"

"We can't even get help," Blink twittered. "The astro-jet isn't picking us up until tomorrow morning."

"Then we will just have to help ourselves," Teggs declared. He thought hard. "We must try to scare those monsters away – or at least slow them down."

Dutch gulped. "I guess all we can do is try, right?"

"Right." Teggs looked at the ripped, rubbery orange tent and began to smile. "Tell me, guys, have you ever met the Dreaded Eight-Legged Rock-Spitting Blob Monster?"

"Er, no," Blink admitted, and Dutch shook his head.

"Neither have I," said Teggs. "But I think it's time those T. rexes did!" Teggs grinned at his puzzled friends. "Blink, you're the fastest. Fly back to the camp and warn everyone. They must clear out double-quick."

"OK, Teggs," said Blink, blinking like crazy.

"While you're gone, Dutch and I will turn this tent into a creepy costume," Teggs explained. "We will dress up as a Rock-Spitting Blob Monster!"

"Wow," Dutch gasped. "That plan rocks!"

Blink shook his head. "You mean, that plan *spits* rocks – at the T. rexes!"

"Right!" Teggs looked at his two friends. "We've got a deadly dangerous job to do, dinos . . . Do we dare?"

Blink and Dutch put their own hands on top of Teggs's. "WE DARE!" they all cried.

As Blink flapped away at top speed, Teggs picked up the orange tent. "I'll get to work on this," he said. "Dutch, go and collect some rocks, as big as you can carry."

"Will do," said Dutch. "Let's hope those scaly suckers get such a fright, they run far away from the camp and never come back!"

Soon, Dutch and Teggs were struggling into the home-made monster suit. Teggs had dug up some chalk and mud and used it to draw a frightening face on one end of the deflated rubber. Then he had cut out some eyeholes to see through and also a flap so they could throw rocks at their unwelcome visitors. The rocks were balanced between the spikes on Teggs's back so Dutch could reach them easily.

"Do you think we look scary enough?" said Dutch.

"Don't forget, we will also be roaring, spitting rocks and running about on eight legs," said Teggs. "What could be scarier? Let's get going!"

Reaching the right place wasn't easy. It was hot and squashed inside the costume. Teggs and Dutch couldn't see very well, so they kept tripping up and walking into trees. The wind almost knocked them over several times. The rocks on Teggs's back made his spikes ache.

"T. rex valley coming up," Dutch whispered at last. "They were right at the bottom when we left them . . ."

But suddenly, Teggs saw movement in the undergrowth ahead. The butterflies in his tummy turned into bats as six savage T. rexes burst from the bushes! They stared in surprise at the orange blobby monster in front of them.

"They must have climbed out!" Dutch whispered.

"Quick, make like a monster," said Teggs. "ROOAAAAAAR!" he bellowed.

Dutch snatched some rocks from Teggs's back and threw them out of the mouth-flap. "GRROO AAARRR!" The two of them stamped about in their costume, growling till their throats hurt.

The T. rexes just stood there.

"Lord Slyme!" growled the T. rex in flying goggles. "Me thinks us find eight-legged rock-spitting blob monster!"

Lord Slyme snapped his jaws. "Good. Now us *eat* it!"

With a hungry hiss, the terrifying giants stomped towards Teggs and Dutch . . .

Chapter Seven

RACE AGAINST TIME

Terribly tired and scared out of his scales, Blink flew on towards the main camp through the driving wind. "Can't give up," he told himself. "Mustn't give up . . ."

Finally, he flapped out of the sky and flopped down in front of Damona's cave, gasping for breath.

"Clear out!" he squawked.

"Beak-face?" Damona poked her two-horned head out of the cave and frowned. "What are you doing back? Did you get lost?"

"Get everyone out of the camp," the dino-bird panted. "T. rexes close by!"

"T. rexes?" Damona looked shocked. Netta and Splatt peeped out from behind her.

"Teggs and Dutch are risking their lives right now, trying to scare them away," Blink explained. "But that might not work. Everyone must pack up and head north, quickly!"

"Oh, *I* get it . . ." Damona started to smirk. "Nice try, Blink."

Netta nodded. "You can stop pretending now."

"Pretending?" Blink blinked at her furiously. "I'm telling the truth! There *are* T. rexes here!"

"As if," said Splatt. "You're just trying to scare us out so you can get this cool cave back."

"Who cares about a dumb cave?" Blink squawked.

"You do," said Damona. "Now push off!"

"You have to believe me, you two-horned twit!" Blink shouted. Then he flapped down the hillside to where a trio of triceratops sat beneath a tree.

"Please, guys, listen. We have to clear the camp, quickly. There are T. rexes—"

"Don't listen to him!" Netta yelled. "He's trying to pinch your camp for himself."

"I'm not!" Blink protested.

But the three triceratops gave him a dirty look and stalked away.

Desperately, Blink hopped over to a lime-coloured lambeosaur. "Will you help me clear the camp before the T. rexes sniff it out?"

"T. rexes indeed," the lambeosaur said stuffily.

Blink flapped up and down helplessly. "No one will believe me!" he cried. "Oh, help. What am I going to do?"

"CATCH ORANGE MONSTER THING! *EAT IT!*"

Lord Slyme's screech echoed through the air as Teggs and Dutch hurtled through the wilderness in their tattered tent costume. Teggs's heart was pounding. His mouth was dry. A stitch burned in his side. But he wouldn't stop running, and neither would Dutch.

Trouble was, the drooling T. rexes wouldn't stop either. Which meant that Teggs and Dutch would end up leading them straight to the cadet camp! Every time they tried to change direction, another of the ravenous 'rexes mashed through the spindly undergrowth and blocked their way, forcing them back onto the main path.

"What do we do?" Dutch panted, as they ran along the edge of a cliff. "If we get too tired, we get eaten!"

Teggs grinned weakly. "Let's not get too tired!"

Ahead of them, the cliff path curved sharply past a huge boulder. But as they took the turn, Dutch stumbled and slipped out of the costume – and over the cliff edge!

"Dutch!" Teggs yelled, skidding to a stop.

"It's OK!" Dutch's head popped back into view. "There's a ledge down here. We can hide till they go past!"

Teggs jumped down to join Dutch, who hid inside the costume again – just as the hunting T. rexes raced round the corner and pounded past. They did not realize their prey had given them the slip.

"Phew!" said Dutch.

"But those meatheads are still heading for the camp," Teggs reminded him. "I only hope Blink has got the cadets clear by now—Whoops!"

Suddenly, a big gust of wind blew under the tent and knocked them both off the ledge!

"Looks like we're going for an unexpected trip," cried Dutch. "*Whoooaaaa!*"

Helpless, the two friends tumbled down the steep slope of the cliff. Luckily, the tent-costume's rubbery material protected them from the worst bumps. With a roll, a bump, two triple somersaults and a thump, they finally reached the bottom.

"What a ride," groaned Dutch, shaking off bits of tent. "Even my bruises have bruises."

"But look," said Teggs shakily, pointing past a clump of trees. "I think we found a shortcut . . ."

On the other side of the trees were a dozen more bright orange tents. It was the cadet camp!

"Come on!" Dutch pulled Teggs back to his feet and they limped towards it.

But when they arrived, they couldn't believe their eyes. Everyone was still here! Some dinosaurs were exploring, some were reading, some were toasting marshmallows without a care in the world.

And there was Blink, flapping about like crazy. "The T. rexes *are* coming!" he kept squawking. "It's true!"

"Yes, it is!" Teggs yelled.

Suddenly, everyone stopped what they were doing and stared.

"Teggs, I'm so sorry!" said Blink, flapping over to his side. "No one will listen. Damona told everyone I was playing a trick to get our cave back!"

Even as he spoke, Damona strolled out of the cave and noticed Teggs and Dutch. "Hey, what happened to you two?" she called. "You look awful! You look like you went ten rounds with a . . ." Her face went pale. "With a *T. rex*?"

"Six of them, to be precise," said Teggs gravely. "They are very big and very fast – and they will be here any minute!"

Chapter Eight

THE BIG, FAT BATTLE

"You heard Teggs," Dutch shouted at the astrosaur cadets. "We need to get out of here, dudes. *Scram!*"

The cadets stared at Teggs and Dutch in alarm and amazement. Then they burst into action, deflating their tents and packing up their camps.

Damona came running up to Teggs with Netta and Splatt. "I'm sorry," she

said. "I thought you were playing a joke on us. Blink would have got everyone safely away long ago if it wasn't for me."

"Never mind that now," said Teggs. "You were super-fast at clearing everyone out of the hall yesterday. Do you think you can do the same here?"

"I'll do it even *faster* with my team to help me," Damona promised.

Netta and Splatt were already on the case. "Come on, you lot!" boomed Netta, while Splatt whizzed about like a sheepdog herding sheep. "You can all hide in our cave. It's very deep."

"I'm not sure that will work!" said Blink, blinking. "I've read all about T. rexes. Once those meat-scoffing monsters smell a meal, they won't rest till they've eaten it. Our only chance is to run away and stay far enough ahead of them!"

"Maybe not our *only* chance," breathed Teggs. He was watching one of the plump orange tents deflate. It went from a bungalow-sized balloon to a fat lump of rubber in seconds.

"I've got an idea – but it's very, very dangerous. Who will help me stand up to those monsters?"

"I will," said Dutch.

"And me!" trilled Blink.

Damona stepped forward. "My uncle sorted out the T. rexes, and so will I!"

Teggs called out to the camp. "OK, I need two more volunteers."

A large, grey triceratops called Trebor and a gum-chewing girl sauropelta called Akk broke away from the line of dinosaurs queuing at the cave. "We will help too," Trebor said.

"I'll organize everyone in the cave," Splatt offered.

"And we will be standing by to help you if things go wrong," Netta promised.

"OK, guys," said Teggs. "Here's what we do . . ."

Five minutes later, Teggs and his helpers were waiting nervously for their face-off with the ravenous 'rexes. Teggs wasn't sure he would hear them coming over the pounding of his heart.

"My uncle fought T. rexes with dung-torpedoes and laser-blasters at the Battle of Belliflop." Damona sighed and looked down at the bright, rubbery bundles in her arms. "What have we got? Tents!"

"You know what to do," Teggs murmured.

"Yes." Blink clutched a small pile of deflated tents to his chest. "And our timing must be perfect."

Dutch nodded. "A second too late and it's, 'Hello, T. rex tum' time!'"

Suddenly, they felt the ground tremble under their feet, and heard heavy footsteps crashing towards them.

"Good luck, everyone," Teggs whispered.

The next moment, with an ear-splitting roar, all six T. rexes smashed through the nearby bushes. At the sight of the plant-eaters their piggy eyes grew wide as saucers. Their little arms twitched. Their big jaws dribbled.

Lord Slyme pushed to the front of the
scaly scrum. "What have us here?" he
hissed. "A juicy jumble of jelly-soft dino-
dinners! Me a *brilliant* hunter!"

"Brilliant?" Teggs scoffed, as Slyme
stamped towards him. "I think you've
got an *inflated* opinion of yourself!"

The horrible hunter opened his jaws to bite him in half. But Teggs hurled the tent into Slyme's mouth and yanked on the black cord. The tent puffed up in a moment – and so did Slyme's throat!

"*MRRRRPH!*" he spluttered, his little arms waving in the air. It looked as if he had swallowed a space-hopper!

Angrily – but also stupidly – the other T. rexes attacked in the same way. Dutch dumped his tent in the mouth of one of them and yanked on the cord. Its head inflated like a big balloon!

Another tried to catch Blink. But Blink flapped into the air. As the T. rex looked up, Blink dropped three tents down its neck and pulled the strings. The monster's stomach swelled up and it bounced about helplessly.

Trebor dealt with another T. rex just as Dutch had. But Akk was not so lucky. Her tent inflated by accident before she could get it into anyone's mouth. Two 'rexes charged towards her . . .

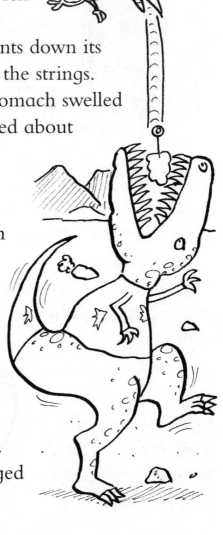

"Teggs!" shouted Damona. "Let's play skittles!"

Teggs took one look at the T. rex with the round, inflated tummy and understood what she meant. Together, the two cadets whacked the evil hunter with their tails. They sent it rolling like a giant, scaly bowling ball! It knocked over the two T. rexes before they could grab Akk. Akk quickly jumped on their heads and knocked them senseless.

That left just one T. rex standing. But it was the fastest of all. It darted forward and sank its teeth into Teggs's tail!

"*Yeeeowwww!*" Teggs yelled, as powerful jaws lifted him into the air . . .

"All charge!" yelled Dutch.

He, Damona, Trebor and Akk ran at the T. rex at the same time. They smashed into its scaly stomach and sides. The T. rex gasped. Teggs slipped from its jaws and tumbled to the ground.

At the same moment, Blink swooped down and chucked another two saggy tents into the monster's mouth.

"*URRPH!*" spluttered the T. rex. Its jaws were yanked open as the tents inflated, and its eyes nearly popped from its head! It staggered back, tripped over Lord Slyme's oversized neck and crashed to the floor.

"We beat them!" cried Trebor, grabbing Akk in a hug.

"But what about Teggs?" cried Blink. "He's not moving!"

Blink, Dutch and Damona raced to the stegosaur's side. But was it too late . . . ?

Chapter Nine

A SNAPPY SOUVENIR

"Dude!" Dutch crouched over Teggs.
"Wake up. Your plan totally worked!"
"Please wake up," Blink added.
"You're the most daring dino of all. You
can't leave us!"

"Yeah, come on, you dumb, brave stegosaur," said Damona, nudging his cheek with her horns. "You *must* be all right. If you're not, I will never forgive you!"

Teggs's eyes flickered open. "I . . . I . . ."

"He's alive!" Blink turned a somersault. "Yay!"

"Shh," said Damona, straining to hear. "He's trying to say something."

"I . . . think . . ." Teggs raised his head weakly to look at her – then grinned. "I think you're standing on my foot!"

"Teggs!" She scowled, backing away. "I thought you were hurt."

"I'm fine now!" Teggs cried, bouncing up and hugging his friends. "Apart from some tooth-marks in my tail. Well done, all of you."

"Hooray!" yelled Netta, leading the other cadets from the cave. They all burst into applause.

"You've turned T. rex into T. *wrecks*!" Splatt cried, dancing round the scaly monsters as they lay groaning on the ground. "Let's tie them up, quickly."

Damona frowned. "But we don't have any ropes."

"Then we must find some," said Teggs. "All of us!"

The cadets worked as a team. Some dug up tough tree roots. Some went to their first-aid kits and knotted bandages together. The T. rexes only had small arms  so they were quite easy to tie up. One lambeosaur even found a giant snake! It coiled itself around Lord Slyme's legs and arms very happily, gripping them tight. The T. rex wriggled helplessly in the serpent's grip.

"No one treats me like this," snarled Lord Slyme with some difficulty. "No one!"

"*We* do," said Teggs. "The cadets of Astrosaurs Academy!"

Suddenly, the sound of huge engines filled the air. Everyone stared in astonishment as a giant craft swished down from the sky.

"It's the astro-jet!" Teggs yelled, as the mighty space-plane landed close by.

A moment later, Commander Gruff stuck his head out through the doors, an unripe banana clamped in his mouth as always. "Looks like you new recruits had a little trouble here."

"Nothing we couldn't handle, sir," said Teggs, smiling at Damona.

"We worked together and got the job done," Damona agreed. "Although obviously *I* was best—" Dutch nudged her in the ribs. "Ow!"

"How come you came back for us early, sir?" asked Blink.

"When those T. rexes crashed they sent a call for help to their home planet," Gruff revealed.

"Right!' Dutch turned to Blink. "We heard them say they would, remember?"

"Well, we picked up their signal and came flying to get them," said Gruff. "But it seems we wasted our time!"

"I don't think so, sir," said Teggs, smiling at his friends. "The sooner this lot get off Astro Prime, the better!"

"Us agree," moaned the T. rex with the inflated stomach. "Us *definitely* agree!"

Commander Gruff took charge and things were soon sorted out. Lord Slyme and his slaves were sent back to Teerex Major with a warning never to return to plant-eater space. And more astro-jets arrived to take Teggs and all his fellow cadets back to Astrosaurs Academy.

Teggs was exhausted. He slept for twenty-four hours. When he woke up his tail was throbbing – but otherwise he felt fine. In fact he was so hungry he ate his mattress! Then he, Blink and Dutch went to the Learning Zone for their afternoon class.

"Oh, no!" Blink squawked.

"What's up, dude?" Dutch wondered.

He shook his beak. "In all the excitement, we never got anything for show-and-tell!"

"Bad luck, Teggs!" Damona smirked. "Looks like you might not be getting your Planet Explorer's medal after all!"

Teggs's heart sank. "Damona's right. We haven't completed our mission!"

Netta giggled, and Splatt pulled out a giant pine cone from under his desk. "We brought back this. It's bound to win the special prize!"

Just then, Commander Gruff stomped into the classroom. Everyone saluted.

"OK," Gruff said impatiently. "You had some unexpected action in your camp yesterday, but it's time to get back to business. We will start with show-and-tell."

"Oh, no!" groaned Dutch.

Every team had something to show. Damona's Darlings had their giant pine cone. The Triceratops Troop produced a perfect pink eggshell. The Leaf-Loving Squad pulled out a funny-shaped stick . . . and so it went on.

"Hmm, not bad," said Gruff, as Trebor showed off a fossil spider.
"And what about the Daring Dinos? What have *you* got?"

"Um . . ." Blink blinked so hard he blew some paper off his desk. "We seem to have . . . accidentally . . . er . . ."

"Forgotten to get anything," Dutch concluded.

You could have heard a pin drop in the quiet classroom. Teggs felt dreadful.

Gruff cleared his throat. "You were very brave in the wilderness, boys, and I am proud of you all." He sighed. "But I

cannot break the rules. If you did not
bring back anything to show and tell,
you have failed the mission – and I
cannot give you your Planet Explorer
medals."

"Wait!" squawked Blink. And he
pecked at the bony barbs at the end of
Teggs's tail.

"Ow!" Teggs yelped. "What was that
for?"

Dutch grinned. "Looks like you *did* bring something back after all, dude!"

Blink opened his beak – and Teggs  saw a large, ivory spike lying there. He grinned. "A T. rex tooth! It must have got stuck in my tail when that monster bit me."

"Cool!" cried Trebor, and the rest of the class joined in with *oohs* and *ahhs*.

"I suppose it's *quite* a good show-and-tell," said Damona huffily. But then she managed a smile. "OK. It's brilliant."

"Indeed it is!" Commander Gruff grinned. "In fact – it's going to win the special prize – a whole starship full of fresh food to chomp on."

"*Wheeeee!*" cried Blink, as Dutch gave him and Teggs a high-five.

"And everyone can join in the feast,"
Teggs declared. "We will have a party in
the dino-dorms tonight!" Damona,
Netta and Splatt led the cheering that
followed, and Teggs beamed round at his
fellow cadets. "We've made it through
our first mission at Astrosaurs Academy
. . . and I can't wait to find out what
we'll be getting up to next!"

THE END

ASTROSAURS ACADEMY
CONTEST CARNAGE!
STEVE COLE

Young Teggs stegosaur is a pupil at **ASTROSAURS ACADEMY** – where dinosaurs train to be **ASTROSAURS!** With his best friends Blink and Dutch beside him, amazing adventures and far-out-fun are never far away!

Teggs and his fellow astro-cadets can't wait to compete in a brand new sports tournament on the Academy's doorstep – the Megasaur Challenge! But when several athletes are injured in a number of nutty "accidents", the contest is plunged into chaos. Suspecting foul play, Teggs investigates. But will he survive long enough to learn the terrifying truth?

ISBN: 978 1 862 30555 7

COWS IN ACTION

THE TER-MOO-NATORS
STEVE COLE

Genius cow Professor McMoo and his trusty sidekicks, Pat and Bo, are the star agents of the C.I.A. – short for COWS IN ACTION! They travel through time, fighting evil bulls from the future and keeping history on the right track . . .

When Professor McMoo invents a brilliant time machine, he and his friends are soon attacked by a terrifying TER-MOO-NATOR – a deadly robo-bull who wants to mess with the past and change the future! And that's only the start of an incredible adventure that takes McMoo, Pat and Bo from a cow paradise in the future to the scary dungeons of King Henry VIII . . .

It's time for action.

COWS IN ACTION

ISBN: 978 1 862 30189 4

Astrosaurs
THE SUN-SNATCHERS
STEVE COLE

Teggs is no ordinary
dinosaur – he's an
ASTROSAUR!
Captain of the
amazing spaceship DSS *Sauropod*,
he goes on dangerous missions and
fights evil – along with his faithful
crew, Gipsy, Arx and Iggy!

A world of woolly rhinos is
in desperate peril – one of their three
suns has gone missing! Racing to the
rescue, Teggs and his team must fight
a gigantic star-swallowing menace
before theother two suns get snatched
away. And all the time, other
dangers are drawing closer . . .

ISBN: 978 1 862 30254 9

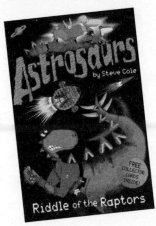

Astrosaurs

RIDDLE OF THE RAPTORS

STEVE COLE

Teggs is no ordinary
dinosaur – he's an
ASTROSAUR!

Captain of the amazing spaceship DSS
Sauropod, he goes on dangerous missions
and fights evil – along with his faithful
crew, Gypsy, Arx and Iggy!

When a greedy gang of meat-eating
raptors raid the *Sauropod* and kidnap
two top athletes, Teggs and his crew race
to the rescue. But there's more to the
raptors' plot than meets the eye. Can
Teggs solve their rascally riddle in time?

ISBN: 978 0 099 47294 0